CATHERINE GOWER
lived and worked in China from 1997 to 1999,
teaching English and learning Mandarin and Chinese calligraphy.
She is now an editor in the English Language Teaching
Division of Oxford University Press.
This is her first children's book.

HE ZHIHONG
was born in China in 1970 and graduated
from Beijing Academy of Fine Arts, where she studied
traditional Chinese painting. She paints on both silk and rice paper.
He Zhihong now lives in Paris and has several books published
in France. *Contes des peuples de Chine*, received the Nuit du Livre award
for the best children's book. This is her first book
for Frances Lincoln.

For my parents – C.G.
For Guillaume and my parents – H.Zh.

LONG-LONG'S
NEW YEAR

A Story about
the Chinese Spring Festival

Catherine Gower
Illustrated by **He Zhihong**

FRANCES LINCOLN CHILDREN'S BOOKS

"Hey, Long-Long! Wake up,
we're almost there!"
　　Long-Long peeped out over
the baskets of Grandpa's juicy cabbages.
It was his first time ever to ride to town.
He'd never seen so many people, talking, walking,
cycling and exercising to their favourite music.
Spring Festival was in the air!

Suddenly, there was a loud POP!

"*Aiya!*" cried Grandpa as he looked at the cart's flat tyre.

"I'll push, you pull!" said Long-Long.

The sun was already high in the sky, and they had to hurry to arrive at the market before the customers!

Grandpa was anxious to sell his cabbages
so their family would have money for Spring Festival.
They unloaded the baskets, then Long-Long set off
to find a bicycle repair shop.

"Aiya!" shrieked a lady wobbling on her bicycle, balancing oranges and a lively fish she'd bought for her lunch.

She headed straight for Long-Long, braking just in time. The fish flopped out of the lady's basket. Oranges flew everywhere and Long-Long darted about, scooping them up and putting them back in the basket. The lady gave Long-Long a big lipstick smile and handed him an orange.

It was only then that he noticed they'd stopped right outside the bicycle repair shop!

The repairman patched the tube and put it back inside Grandpa's tyre. Now other people were waiting for repairs.

"Shall I help for a while?" asked Long-Long.

"Good idea!" said the repairman. "How about pumping some tyres?"

Long-Long pushed down on the pump with all his strength. Each of his customers dropped three or four *mao* coins into a wooden box. The repairman thanked Long-Long, pressing a shiny new silver *yuan* coin into his hand.

"Long-Long, you're back!"
Grandpa smiled, but Long-Long
saw that the baskets were still full.
"Don't worry, Grandpa.
The bicycle's repaired. And look,
I got an orange, and I made
some money!"
Grandpa looked at the shiny coin
in Long-Long's hand. "You're a good
grandson, Long-Long, but this coin
won't buy all the food for Spring Festival."
Long-Long felt sad. He and Grandpa
had patiently counted the days until the cabbages
were ready for market. Ma and little cousin
Hong-Hong would be disappointed if they
brought home only a cartload of wilted leaves!

Close by, an old woman was selling cabbages too,
but hers weren't as fresh as Grandpa's. When nobody
was looking she sprinkled the leaves with water
to make them look fresher!

The old woman called out to passers-by before they even reached Grandpa's baskets. She waved her cabbage leaves under their noses, and weighed them quickly. The cheated townsfolk didn't notice the holes and dust!

Long-Long wandered off, trying
to think what to do. Soon he arrived
at a street restaurant. The smells
from the cook's pan were wonderful.

"Hey, are you hungry?" shouted the cook.

Long-Long looked at his silver coin. What should he buy? Two steamed buns stuffed with pork and ginger… no, rice soup with pickled vegetables… Then Long-Long remembered Ma and little Hong-Hong. He put the coin back in his pocket.

"I've never seen you around here," said the cook.

"I came with Grandpa to sell cabbages," answered Long-Long quietly.

"Then sell me fresh cabbage for my soup and steamed buns!" she said.

Long-Long led the cook back to Grandpa. He was worried that she would buy cabbages from the old woman instead, but when she saw the old woman, the cook shouted angrily, "I told you never to come back here! What are you selling this time? More holes and caterpillars?"

A crowd gathered round to see what was happening,
and soon everybody was buying from Grandpa.
He weighed the leaves carefully, then Long-Long tied them
like bunches of flowers to present to the customers.

The old woman couldn't stand it. She spat and hissed
and stamped her feet, but this didn't help her sell
any more cabbages!

"Long-Long, we've sold every single leaf!" called Grandpa.
"Now we have all the money we need for Spring Festival!"
    They bought spices, rice, flour and cooking oil, firecrackers
and lucky words like *fu* painted on red paper. Everything went
into the cart, except for a huge salted fish. There wasn't room,
so Grandpa tied it to the handlebars!
    Then he stopped outside the *Hundred Goods Store*
        and handed 10 yuan to Long-Long. "Go and treat yourself,"
            said Grandpa, "while I tie everything down into the cart
                for the journey home."

Inside the Hundred Goods Store, a mother was buying bows for her little girl's hair. Long-Long thought of Hong-Hong and bought two that were shaped like strawberries. They'd be perfect for Hong-Hong's plaits and would match her rosy-red cheeks.

Red was also the colour of Ma's hands when they were cold. Long-Long chose hand cream for Ma, but the rest of Grandpa's 10 yuan wasn't quite enough. If only he had one more yuan…

And then Long-Long remembered – the coin in his pocket from
the bicycle repairman! He held it out proudly to the shop assistant.
Suddenly, the beating of a gong and a roll of drums came
from a procession passing by outside. Long-Long ran to see!

Back at the cart, Grandpa was waiting for Long-Long. He was holding a stick of toffee fruit. "I've bought you a *tang-hu-lu*," he said. "Let's go home now, Long-Long. Ma and Hong-Hong are busy preparing our own Spring Festival!"

As Grandpa and Long-Long rode home,
they saw flashes of red paper on the doors
and in the windows of the houses.

"Chop! Chop! Chop!" they heard as they arrived home.
Ma was preparing dumplings for dinner.

Hong-Hong came running out. "They're back! They're back!"
she shouted, and Ma appeared at the door.

Long-Long took a square of red paper with fu painted on it.
He pinned it, upside down, to the front door. Ma and Grandpa
smiled and Hong-Hong clapped. Happiness and good luck
had arrived in Long-Long's home just in time for Spring Festival.

THE VERY FIRST
CHINESE SPRING FESTIVAL

Far back in time there was a village just like Long-Long's, but the people there lived in fear. Every twelve months a terrible monster called *Nian* came up from his den on the sea-bed to torment the villagers. One year, as they fled to the mountains to escape, they passed a beggar on his way to the village, but nobody stopped to warn him. The only person left at home was an old widow, too tired to run after the others. She invited the beggar in and told him about the monster. The beggar offered his help, but first he asked the old widow to cook him some dumplings as he was very hungry.

Chop! Chop! Chop! As the widow prepared vegetables for the dumplings, Nian awoke from his long, deep dreams and approached the village. Sleepy-headed, he was irritated by the chopping noise the old widow made. He charged towards her house, but the beggar was ready for him. Red paper, which the beggar had pinned to the doors and windows, flashed across Nian's sensitive eyes. They felt as though they'd been stabbed by a thousand needles! Then the beggar set fire to a magic baton of bamboo. Crackle! Spit! Hiss! Nian's delicate ears couldn't stand the noise. He fled back to the bottom of the sea, and the beggar disappeared.

When the villagers returned from the mountain, the old widow told them the beggar's advice. Since then, Chinese people have followed his example every Spring Festival. The only difference is that nowadays, people don't have magic bamboo batons to scare Nian away. What do you think Long-Long's family will use instead?

Chinese words in the story

Long	龙	This is the Chinese word for dragon. Long-Long got his name because he was born in the Chinese Year of the Dragon.
Aiyu!	哎呀	Chinese people cry out this word when they are surprised or upset.
Mao	毛	This is Chinese money. Mao come in notes or coins. 1 mao is worth a bit less than 1 penny.
Yuan	元	This is also Chinese money, and there are 10 mao in 1 yuan. Yuan also come in notes and coins. 1 yuan is worth a little bit less than 10 pence.
Ma	妈	Chinese children call their mothers Ma.
Hong	红	This is the Chinese word for the colour red. Hong-Hong got her name because of her two rosy-red cheeks!
Fu	福	This word means good luck. It is often painted on red paper. Chinese people stick the paper upside-down on their front doors to bring them luck for the New Year.
Hundred Goods Store	百货大楼	This is a traditional department store found in lots of Chinese towns. It sells everything you can imagine!
Tang-hu-lu	糖葫芦	This is a kind of sweet. Small round fruit are held on a stick. The fruit are covered in melted toffee and look like baby toffee apples. A tang-hu-lu is a treat for Chinese children.
Nian	年	According to Chinese legend, Nian is a terrible monster. It is also the Chinese word for 'year'. Every Spring Festival, Chinese people get rid of the old Nian in time to start the New Year.

Teddybear Blue

Malachy Doyle

Illustrated by Christina Bretschneider

Teddybear Blue is always disappearing!
His owner wants to cuddle him but he's run off to play
hide-and-seek, or he's in a cupboard, or he's in the park.
Yet, however good or bad he may be,
no toy is as special as Teddybear Blue.

ISBN 1-84507-126-3

Fly on the Wall: Roman Fort

Mick Manning and Brita Granström

Patrol with a windswept centurion,
eavesdrop in the smelly toilets, visit a tasty Roman banquet,
listen to the crowd as gladiators fight –
you can even meet the Roman emperor!

ISBN 1-84507-124-7

The King with Horse's Ears

Eric Maddern

Illustrated by Paul Hess

No one knows about King Mark's ears except his barber.
Keeping the secret eventually drives him to the doctor,
who advises him to whisper it to the ground.
But sooner or later, the truth will out…

ISBN 0-7112-2079-4

Frances Lincoln titles are available from all good bookshops.
You can also buy books and find out more about your favourite titles, authors
and illustrators on our website: www.franceslincoln.com